Magic Kitten

Classroom Chaos

Brian—the shy blue twin.

GROSSET & DUNLAP
Published by the Penguin Group
Penguin Group (USA) Inc., 375 Hudson Street,
New York, New York 10014, USA
Penguin Group (Canada), 90 Eglinton Avenue East, Suite 700,
Toronto, Ontario M4P 2Y3, Canada
(a division of Pearson Penguin Canada Inc.)
Penguin Books Ltd., 80 Strand, London WC2R 0RL, England
Penguin Group Ireland, 25 St. Stephen's Green, Dublin 2, Ireland
(a division of Penguin Books Ltd.)
Penguin Group (Australia), 250 Camberwell Road,
Camberwell, Victoria 3124, Australia
(a division of Pearson Australia Group Pty. Ltd.)
Penguin Books India Pvt. Ltd., 11 Community Centre, Panchsheel Park,
New Delhi—110 017, India
Penguin Group (NZ), 67 Apollo Drive, Rosedale, North Shore 0632, New Zealand
(a division of Pearson New Zealand Ltd.)
Penguin Books (South Africa) (Pty.) Ltd., 24 Sturdee Avenue,
Rosebank, Johannesburg 2196, South Africa

Penguin Books Ltd., Registered Offices:
80 Strand, London WC2R 0RL, England

Text copyright © 2006 Sue Bentley. Illustrations copyright © 2006 Angela Swan.
Cover illustration copyright © 2006 Andrew Farley. First printed in Great Britain in
2006 by Penguin Books Ltd. First published in the United States in 2008 by Grosset
& Dunlap, a division of Penguin Young Readers Group, 345 Hudson Street, New
York, New York 10014. GROSSET & DUNLAP is a trademark of Penguin Group
(USA) Inc. Printed in the U.S.A.

Library of Congress Cataloging-in-Publication Data is available.

ISBN 978-0-448-44999-9   10 9 8

Magic Kitten

Classroom Chaos

SUE BENTLEY

Illustrated by Angela Swan

Grosset & Dunlap

★ Prologue ★

As Cirrus and Prince Flame hid in a cave, the old lion sensed something strange. "Your uncle is close by, Prince Flame. You must disguise yourself again! It isn't safe for you to be here," Cirrus called to the young lion.

Flame's fur crackled with silver sparks. There was a dazzling white flash and suddenly the lion disappeared. In his place now stood a tiny, fluffy, black-and-white kitten.

Cirrus leaned down and brushed his old gray muzzle against the top of the kitten's fluffy head. "You must go back to the other world, Prince Flame. But stay in this kitten disguise. It will serve you well and keep you hidden from your evil uncle."

Suddenly Flame and Cirrus heard a menacing growl. Flame looked up at Cirrus with his emerald-green eyes. "Uncle Ebony rules my kingdom. One day I will return and claim my throne!" he meowed bravely.

Cirrus's worn teeth flashed in a brief smile. "Yes you will, my prince. But only once your magic powers have become stronger. But for now, you must go and hide!" he cried.

Just as Flame scrambled to hide behind a rock, an enormous adult lion burst through the waterfall in the cave. His huge paws thudded on the ground.

"Cirrus! Tell me where my nephew is hiding! I must find him," Ebony demanded.

Flame's tiny body trembled in fear as he listened from behind the rock.

Cirrus growled. "Prince Flame is far away now. You will never find him!" he responded.

Ebony roared with rage. "My spies are looking for him. Flame cannot hide from me forever . . ."

Behind the rock, Flame felt the magic power building inside him. He let out a tiny meow as silver sparks ignited in his black-and-white fur. The cave began to fade, and he felt himself falling. The magic had worked once more . . .

Chapter
ONE

"Bye! See you at the end of the semester!" Abi West called to her parents from the upstairs window.

As the car pulled out of Brockinghurst School's parking lot, Abi turned back to her new room. She felt excited but a little nervous. It was going to be strange to share a room with someone she didn't know.

"Might as well unpack," she decided, lifting her suitcase onto one of the beds.

There were two single beds with blue

quilts and night tables. Blue-checked
curtains and a red rug made the room
bright and cozy.

From the window, she saw that more
cars were pulling into the front parking

lot. Girls in uniform were getting out
and saying good-bye to their families.

Abi had just finished putting away her
clothes and books when the door crashed
open with a bang.

A pretty, fair-haired girl marched into
the room. She scowled at Abi. "Who are
you?"

"Hi," Abi said. "I'm Abi West."

"Well, you're in my room," the girl
said rudely.

"I thought I could choose any room,"
Abi said. "I just put all my stuff away."

The other girl put her hands on her
hips. "And I'm supposed to care? You'll
just have to move it then!"

Abi blinked at her, unsure what to
do. The other girl looked about eleven, a

year older than Abi.

"I thought I heard your voice, Keera Moore," said a calm voice from the doorway.

Abi spun around. She saw a tall woman with a pleasant face. It was Mrs. York, the head teacher. There was a small, thin girl with her.

Keera changed completely. "Oh, hello, Mrs. York," she said with a smile. "Abi here was just saying she didn't mind moving to another room."

"No, I wasn't!" Abi said indignantly. "You told me this was your room. And that I had to move out!"

Keera glared at her, her blue eyes flashing. "You little tattletale," she hissed.

"That's enough, Keera," the teacher

said. "You know very well that rooms are never reserved at Brockinghurst." She turned to Abi. "Abi West, I want you to meet Sasha Parekh. I thought it might be a good idea for you two to share this room. You'll both have a lot in common. It's the first time either of you has been away from home."

"Ugh," Keera sneered under her breath.

Abi smiled at Sasha, who was very pretty with dark eyes and olive skin. She wore her thick black hair in a long braid. On one cheek she had a red birthmark.

"It's really nice to meet you," Abi said. Sasha seemed a hundred times nicer than Keera already!

"You too," Sasha said shyly.

"I have some animal posters to put on the wall. Would you like to help me?" Abi asked.

Sasha dark eyes lit up. "Definitely! I love animals."

"So do I. Especially big cats," Abi said, warming to Sasha.

Keera pointed a finger at her open mouth and made pretend gagging sounds.

Mrs. York frowned at her. "This room seems to be taken, Keera. I suggest you try the one next door. It's identical to this one."

"Oh, all right." Keera rolled her eyes as she stomped outside with her suitcase. Mrs. York turned back to Abi and Sasha. "I'll leave you two to settle in. Come down to the hall when you hear the bell. You'll meet your teachers and get your

schedules."

"She's nice, isn't she?" Abi said to
Sasha after Mrs. York had left.

Sasha nodded.

Suddenly a lot of banging came from

the room next door. Then a voice complained, "This is an ugly room! And this school is a smelly dump! I hate being back here!"

Sasha looked at Abi. "Keera!" they said. The two of them began laughing.

"Phew! There's so much to remember," groaned Abi. She sat down next to Sasha at a table in the main hall.

The room had wooden beams and walls of dark, carved wood. An enormous fireplace took up most of the end wall. The room was buzzing with girls and teachers, and everyone seemed to be talking at the same time.

Sasha bit her nails nervously. "I can't remember any of the teachers' names or where the classrooms are."

"I can't either. But I think we'll get used to it soon," Abi said.

"Well! If it isn't the tattletale," a voice behind her said.

Abi didn't need to turn around to know who it was. "Hello, Keera," she said.

Keera came up and leaned her elbows on the table. She was with two other girls. One had brown hair and freckles and the other was tall and thin with black curly hair.

Abi remembered hearing their names called out earlier that day: Marsha Clarke and Tiwa Rhames.

"Did you bring your teddy bears to help you sleep?" Keera said in a mocking, baby voice.

Tiwa snickered. "After all, we wouldn't want you to have nightmares about the ghost."

"What ghost?" asked Abi. "You're making it up. There's no such thing."

Keera smirked. "Oh, no? Haven't you heard about the Gray Lady of Brockinghurst? She haunts the school's hallways, waiting for bratty little first-years. I'd watch out if I were you!" She turned to Marsha and Tiwa. "Come on, let's go and see if the store's open."

The girls nudged each other and laughed as they walked away.

Sasha glanced nervously at Abi. "Do you think there really is a ghost?" she asked. "Most old buildings are supposed to be haunted, aren't they?"

Abi smiled at her as she gathered up all the papers she'd been given. "Keera was just trying to scare us. Don't look so worried." She turned to her backpack. "Oh, I forgot the folder for our next class. I'll just run upstairs and get it."

"Okay. I'll wait here," Sasha said, looking more relaxed now.

Abi found the nearest doorway and went out of the hall. Hurrying past a row of classrooms, she found a narrow stairway. Five minutes later, after countless twists and turns, Abi stopped on a gloomy landing.

"Oh, great! I'm totally lost," she said aloud.

Abi looked around. Narrow windows

of thick glass were set into the walls. Dust swirled in the shafts of light that managed to get through. In front of her there was an old door, covered with cobwebs. She pushed at it with her fingertips. It slowly creaked open.

She looked into the gloom, where dark shapes were visible. As her eyes adjusted to the darkness, she saw stacks of old furniture. It was just an old storeroom.

Then suddenly Abi caught something out of the corner of her eye—something pale and glowing. She gasped. It must be the Gray Lady!

Frozen where she stood, Abi gradually began to realize the glow wasn't actually human-shaped at all. But what could it be?

She crept farther into the storeroom. Something was lying across two whole chairs. Abi frowned—it looked like a sparkly furry blanket. As she took another step she heard a low rumbling purr.

Abi blinked in disbelief. The "blanket" looked like a young white lion! He was fast asleep.

She stared at the silver sparkles gleaming in the lion's fur. He looked fierce but beautiful. Abi's heart beat fast. She didn't know whether to stay or run away.

"How did a lion get in here?" she whispered to herself.

The white lion's eyes flew open. He lifted into a crouch. The hair along his back stood up in a spiked ridge.

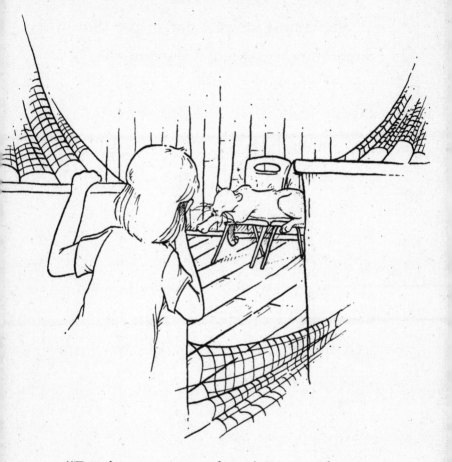

"Don't come any closer! My teeth
are sharp and my claws are strong!" he
growled.

Abi almost jumped out of her skin in terror. "You can talk!" she gasped.

Chapter
TWO

At first the lion just stared at Abi with its piercing emerald eyes.

Abi sensed that it was more frightened than angry. She crouched down to make herself seem smaller. "It's okay. I won't hurt you," she said softly.

The lion relaxed and pricked up its ears. "I do not mean to scare you. I thought you were an enemy," he said in a deep, velvety growl.

"What . . . ? Who are you?" Abi stammered.

"Flame." The lion dipped his head in greeting. "Prince Flame. Heir to the Lion Throne," he told her solemnly.

Abi dipped her head in return. It seemed like the right thing to do. "Where are you from?"

"Far away," Flame replied with a sad look in his eyes.

Abi began to recover from her fear of Flame. She took a step forward and reached her hand out. "I'm Abi. This is my first semester at boarding school. Is it okay if I touch you . . . ?"

"Wait! Stay back!" Flame ordered.

There was a silver flash.

"Oh!" Blinded, Abi put her hands over her eyes. When she looked again, she saw that the white lion had

disappeared. In his place stood a fluffy,
black-and-white kitten with emerald-
green eyes.

"Where's Flame?" Abi gasped.

"I am Flame," the kitten meowed in

a tiny voice. "This is my disguise. I am in hiding. My uncle Ebony is trying to find me. To kill me."

"But why would your uncle want to kill you?" Abi asked.

"He wants to steal my throne. Can you help me, Abi?"

"Of course I will!" She leaned forward and picked up the kitten. "You can live in my room. Just wait until Sasha sees you!"

Flame wriggled. He reached up a tiny paw and touched her chin. "No! You can tell no one. It must be our secret," he urged.

Abi frowned. She felt sure that Sasha could keep a secret.

"You must promise," Flame insisted.

He blinked up at her with wide, trusting eyes.

Abi felt her heart turn over. She didn't want to do anything that put him in danger. "Okay, I promise," she agreed.

Then she had a sudden thought. Students weren't allowed to have pets. How was she going to sneak Flame into her room?

Abi tucked Flame under her sweater. "Sorry. I have to do this," she said as the kitten looked up at her indignantly. "Don't move now, okay?"

Luckily, most of the students were still in the main hall. She managed to find her way back to her room without being seen.

"Here we are," she whispered, putting Flame on her bed.

Flame's eyes scanned the room and then he gave a whiskery grin. "A safe place," he meowed, pointing a black-and-white paw at the bureau.

"You want to go up there?" *It is a good idea*, Abi thought. If he slept at the back against the wall, he'd be out of sight unless someone stood on the bed. "Okay. I'll find something soft to make you a cozy nest."

As Abi began searching in a drawer, Flame's ears pricked. He gave an urgent little meow. "Abi! Someone is coming."

"Oh, no!" Abi whipped around. She saw the door handle turning. There wasn't enough time to hide Flame!

Suddenly Abi felt a strange, tingly feeling down her spine. Silver sparkles leaped from Flame's fur and his whiskers crackled. Little points of light popped in the air around him.

Something very strange was
happening.

Keera stuck her head around the door.
"I thought I heard voices in here." She
looked straight at the bed where Flame
sat!

Abi's breath caught in her throat.
Keera would tell the head teacher about

Flame! Before she could say anything, Keera spoke up.

"I thought so!" Keera's mouth twisted in a triumphant grin. "There's no one else in here! You're such a big baby, Abi West. Wait until I tell everyone that I caught you talking to your imaginary friend!"

Abi looked back at the bed in confusion. Flame sat there large as life, but Keera couldn't see him!

She turned back to Keera. "Tell them what you like! See if I care," she said.

Keera looked disappointed. She turned around and slammed the bedroom door in a huff. Abi heard her walking down the hallway.

Flame began calmly washing his face.

"How come Keera didn't see you?" Abi asked him.

Flame rubbed a paw across his whiskers. "Magic. I choose who sees me," he explained.

"You mean you can make yourself invisible? That's going to make things much easier. It's always really busy in school and since there's no pets allowed, it's probably best if you only show yourself to me. Okay?" Abi grinned at Flame as he nodded that he understood. "This is fantastic! It's going to be so much fun having you here!"

Flame purred back in agreement.

Chapter
THREE

The next few days passed by quickly.
Abi was kept busy with classes, making
new friends, and finding her way around.
She and Sasha got along really well. She
wished Flame could show himself to
Sasha, too, but for Flame's safety and the
sake of the school rules, the fewer people
who knew the better.

Flame came everywhere with her.
During classes, he curled up on a nearby
windowsill or jumped on top of a
bookcase. Abi loved having him around.

He was her special invisible secret. It was
only at night when she lay in bed that
she felt homesick.

Flame snuggled up next to her. Abi
cuddled him and Flame closed his eyes
and purred softly. "Are you homesick,
too?" she whispered, petting his soft fur.

"I miss my good friends." Flame nodded with a sigh.

Abi kissed the top of his head sleepily. It was comforting to hug his warm little body. "We'll just have to look after each other."

Abi awoke one morning to find Sasha already up and dressed. "Yay! It's Saturday! No classes. A day to ourselves," Sasha said, grinning. "What should we do?"

Abi's hands flew to her face. "Yikes! I almost forgot. It's basketball practice! They're choosing teams today." She jumped out of bed and began throwing her clothes on.

Flame sat on the windowsill. The morning sun made his black-and-white coat gleam softly.

"Do you mind if I come?" Sasha asked.

"Of course I don't! But I didn't think you liked basketball," Abi said, stuffing her gym shoes into her sports bag.

Sasha grinned. "I don't! I'm terrible at sports. But I like watching. I can be your number-one fan, if you like!" she joked.

"As if!" Abi laughed and gave her a friendly shove.

Right after breakfast, Abi and Sasha made their way to the school gym. Flame had decided to come, too. He was curled up in Abi's sports bag.

Some other girls from Abi's classes were in the locker room. They called out a greeting to Abi. "Hi!"

"Hi!" Abi answered with a smile. She

changed into her shoes. "Will you be all right?" she whispered to Flame.

"I will be fine. Go and look around," he meowed softly.

Abi ran onto the court where some girls were already practicing their shooting skills. She saw Keera throw the ball straight into the net.

"Good shot," shouted Marsha.

Sasha, who was standing on the sidelines next to Keera's other friend, Tiwa, gave Abi an enthusiastic wave.

Keera looked smug. "In case you didn't know, I'm the school's star shooter," she told Abi.

Miss Green, the gym teacher, blew her whistle. "Gather around, everyone. As you probably know, we play High

Five basketball. So let's divide up into squads. I want to see some teamwork."

Abi put on a jersey with the letters GS, for goal shooter. She really liked High Five. It meant she got a chance to play in all the different positions.

Keera and her friends put on their jerseys. Tiwa said something to Keera, who gave Abi a sly look.

On the whistle, the center passed the ball. Abi and her goal-attack teammate worked to get the ball into the circle. Abi saw an opening. She spun around, aimed, and scored.

"Great job, Abi!" called Sasha.

"Huh! Lucky shot," shouted Tiwa.

Abi scored twice more. She was breathing hard when the timekeeper

called first quarter, but she was eager for
the next game. She loved playing with
her new classmates.

"Switch positions, everyone!" Miss Green called out.

Abi changed to goalkeeper, and on the other team Keera was playing goal attack. She was really good. Abi had to work hard defending against her. Suddenly Keera broke free. She shot at the hoop. The ball bounced off the net.

"Too bad!" called Tiwa.

Keera's face twisted. She looked down at the floor and clenched her fists.

As Abi went after the ball, she saw Flame come bounding up the gym. He jumped on a pile of gym mats. Rolling over, he lay stretched out on his back, showing his pale tummy.

Abi couldn't help chuckling. Flame seemed to be really enjoying himself.

She came and stood behind the line,
ready to throw the ball in.

"Were you laughing at me?" Keera
demanded.

"No," Abi said, puzzled.

Keera scowled. "You'd better not be. I hardly ever miss a shot at the net."

As Abi threw the ball, she suddenly realized that Keera had seen her laughing at Flame. She was going to have to be a lot more careful at keeping him a secret.

Moments later, Keera caught a low pass from Marsha. Abi was watching her closely. As Keera twisted around, she seemed to slip. Her elbow shot out and jabbed into Abi's ribs.

"Oh!" Winded, Abi doubled over in pain.

"She did that on purpose!" Sasha yelled, forgetting to be shy. Her long braid swung around as she jumped up and down in protest.

"Abi's pretending! That didn't hurt," called Tiwa.

Abi held her side, trying to catch her breath.

She heard a low growl. From the corner of her eye, she saw Flame's fur sparkle and his whiskers crackle with electricity. A warm tingling flowed down her spine.

"Uh-oh," breathed Abi. "Now what?"

Keera aimed the ball at the net, gathered herself to jump, then sprang into the air. She threw the ball. Up it went, higher and higher. "No!" she cried as the ball whizzed right up to the roof beams.

Abi watched in amazement as the ball turned slowly in the air and then zoomed downward. It hit Keera on the head.

"Ow!" cried Keera. Suddenly she started to spin around. She spun faster and faster, until she was just a blur!

Chapter
FOUR

The gym erupted with laughter. Sasha laughed, too, her hands over her mouth.

"Help! I can't stop!" Keera wailed, her arms waving around and her gym shoes squeaking as she pirouetted like a skater on ice.

Miss Green made a sound of impatience. "Keera Moore! Do you always have to be the center of attention?"

Abi had caught her breath by now. She held back a grin. No one else could see Flame. There he sat beneath the goalpost, blinking up at Keera. She edged toward him. "Flame," she gently scolded.

"She hurt you, Abi." Flame's eyes glittered mischievously as the silver sparks made a fizzing noise around him and died down.

"I'm okay now," Abi said. "You can stop spinning her now."

Flame hesitated. He pointed a paw at Keera.

Keera came to a sudden stop and stood there swaying gently. "What happened?" she groaned.

Marsha and Tiwa ran over to help her. "Are you all right?"

"Of course I am! Get off me!" snapped Keera, red-faced with embarrassment.

"What a show-off! I bet she feels sick
after all that spinning!" Sasha came over
to Abi.

Miss Green clapped her hands.
"Drama's over! Take a break, everyone.
Gather around. I want to talk to you."

Abi took a cup of water from the
fountain and then went and sat near
Sasha.

"Every year we pick a team captain," Miss Green was saying. "Brockinghurst is hosting a High Five competition at the end of the semester. So it's especially important that our captain is someone who inspires others to do their best . . ."

Keera looked smug. She shifted around as if ready to get up.

". . . so I've decided that this year it'll be—Abi West!"

Keera's jaw dropped. "But—she's only a first year!"

"Stand up, Abi," said Miss Green, frowning at Keera. "I was impressed by the way you played, and you kept a cool head under pressure. That's the kind of captain we need."

"Me?" Abi gasped in surprise as she

rose to her feet. She felt herself blush.

"Well done, Abi," said Miss Green with a warm smile.

Everyone, except Keera and her friends Marsha and Tiwa, clapped and cheered. Sasha shouted loudest of all.

Abi ate her lunch quickly and then hurried to her room.

Once inside, she poured some milk into a saucer. "There you are. It's a special treat," she told Flame.

Flame purred with pleasure. He lapped the milk with his little pink tongue. When he finished drinking, he curled up on her bed and closed his eyes. "I am sleepy now," he meowed softly.

Abi pet him. "Take a nap. I'm going

to the library. I'll see you later." She picked up a folder and tucked it under her arm.

The library was quiet, so Abi had her choice of the computers. She opened her folder and got to work.

Sasha found her there an hour later. "I've been looking everywhere for you." She peered over Abi's shoulder. Her dark eyes opened wide. "Homework? On a Saturday afternoon?"

Abi felt herself get hot. She hesitated, biting her lip. "Sometimes I need to go over things a few times before I understand them," she admitted after a long pause. "I bet you think I'm stupid, don't you?"

Sasha shook her head. "Of course I

don't! Everybody learns in different ways.
Anyway, so what? You're awesome at
sports. I could help you if you like."

"Really? That would be great!" Abi
beamed at her friend. Sasha was great at
schoolwork.

They went through the class notes
together. After another twenty minutes,

Abi sat back. "It makes so much more sense now."

"See, you can do it," Sasha said with a smile. "Do you want to walk into town? We could spend our allowance."

Abi smiled. "Sounds like fun. I'll just put my folder back in our room. Should I meet you at the school gate?"

Sasha nodded.

As Abi hurried out of the library, she saw Marsha coming toward her. Marsha glanced at the folder under Abi's arm but said nothing.

When Abi entered her room, Flame sat up and stretched. He made a little sound of greeting.

"Hello, you." Abi gave him a cuddle. "Did you sleep well? I'm just going into town with Sasha. Do you want to come?"

Flame gave an eager meow. Abi opened her bag and he jumped in.

"Comfortable?" she said, putting on her bag. "Let's go."

Sasha was at the gate. She waved as Abi approached.

It was a warm afternoon. Flame stuck his head out of the bag, enjoying the view as Abi and Sasha walked down the road. The town was a cluster of small houses grouped near an old stone bridge that spanned the river.

"There's the store," Abi said, walking across to a large, thatched cottage that stood by itself. As she and Sasha opened the shop door, a bell rang.

Abi felt Flame jump out of her backpack as he went off looking for exciting smells to explore.

"Oh, no," Sasha whispered. "Look who's over there."

Abi saw Keera flipping through some

magazines. Marsha and Tiwa were at the counter buying chips and drinks.

"Just ignore them. Come on," Abi said, walking toward a display of candy. Sasha followed her. She picked up a bag of lemon drops. "My favorites."

Keera looked up. Abi saw her nudge Marsha and then the three of them drifted over.

Abi's heart sank, but she looked straight at Keera.

"Well, if it isn't the tattletale," Keera jeered. She put her hands on her hips. "Marsha saw you doing extra work. You're just trying to get ahead of everybody in class."

"I'm not!" Abi said. "I'm just trying to keep up."

"Oh, yeah, sure!" Tiwa scoffed.

"Leave her alone. She doesn't have to explain herself to you," Sasha spoke up bravely.

"Who asked you?" Marsha turned to Sasha. "I wouldn't buy any candy if I were you. You might get even more spots!"

Keera and Tiwa laughed.

Sasha hung her head. She put a hand up to cover the birthmark on her cheek.

Abi felt her temper rising. She leaped to her friend's defense. "Leave her alone! She doesn't have spots. It's just a birthmark!"

Marsha jutted her head forward. "Listen to the tattletale sticking up for Spotty. Spo-tty! Spo-tty!" she chanted.

She knocked the bag of candy out of Sasha's hands.

"Oh!" Sasha said with dismay as the bag burst. Candy rolled everywhere.

Abi saw a flash of sparks as Flame leaped onto a nearby shelf. He twitched his whiskers and a fountain of silver sparks shot toward Marsha.

Abi felt her backbone start to prickle. "Uh-oh . . . now what?" she said under her breath.

There was a horrible squeaking noise. First one purple blob appeared on Marsha's cheek, then another. Big blotches began popping up all over Marsha's face!

Chapter
FIVE

Keera and Tiwa stared at Marsha in horror.

"What's wrong with your face?" Tiwa said.

"What do you mean?" Marsha went and looked at herself in the glass window. Her face was completely purple and her nose looked all lumpy, like a blackberry. "Oh no! What's happened to me?" she wailed.

"It's probably the Black Death. Stay away from me!" Keera said.

"It might be contagious!" Tiwa backed away.

Marsha burst into tears.

Abi even felt a little sorry for her. She grabbed Sasha's arm and hurried toward the counter. "Quick! Let's pay for our candy and go!"

Marsha clapped her hands to her face. Moaning, she stumbled past the counter and tried to open the door with her elbow.

"Are you all right, dear?" The store owner looked at her with concern.

"Mnnnff," mumbled Marsha, pulling her school sweater over her head.

Keera and Tiwa dashed for the door. Abi saw Keera grab some bags of candy from the counter while the shopkeeper wasn't looking.

Outside the store, Abi told Sasha what she had seen. "Keera stole them! I saw her shove them in her bag!"

"That's awful. Keera gets a lot of allowance. She was bragging about it at lunch. Those three are so mean." Sasha looked toward Keera and Tiwa who were running down the road. Marsha was walking more slowly, trying to keep her face covered. "It's weird what happened to Marsha, isn't it?" She grinned. "But it serves her right!"

Abi nodded and grinned back. "Yes! But I bet it won't last long. It's probably just an allergy or something."

Sasha still looked puzzled. "Some strange things have been happening at school lately, right?"

"Mmm," Abi said, looking away.

Suddenly they both heard some shouting. It was coming from near the river. A group of boys were pointing up at a tree. Two of them were nudging each other and laughing. One of them, the biggest, who looked like he was thirteen, was collecting stones.

"What are they doing?" Abi said.

Sasha shaded her eyes and looked into the tree. "Oh, no! There's a black-and-white kitten up there."

Abi's heart lurched in her chest. It was Flame!

She realized that Flame must have slipped out of the shop and gone exploring. Climbing the tree had been so exciting that he'd forgotten to stay invisible. Now everyone could see him, so he couldn't do any magic to save himself!

Just then Flame slipped. Abi heard him give a yowl of terror as he only just managed to catch onto a branch hanging out over the river. He clung desperately, his back legs dangling in the air.

"He's going to fall!" Abi gasped. Leaping forward, she raced toward the boys.

The tough-looking boy had grabbed a stone. He drew his arm back and took aim.

"No!" Abi screamed.

She rushed up and shoved the tough-looking boy hard in the chest. He was so surprised that he backed off in amazement.

Abi stood beneath the branch, arms outstretched over the river. She was just in time.

Flame gave a howl and fell out of the tree. Abi caught him, hardly noticing as

his sharp claws scratched her hands and arms.

"I've got you, Flame. You're safe," she whispered. She cradled his trembling body.

The tough boy had recovered from his surprise and his face darkened with anger. "Hey, you!" he shouted at Abi.

"Get her, Craig!" one of the other boys called.

Abi realized that Craig was much bigger than her. She glanced at Sasha, who had just reached the tree. "Run!" she yelled.

Sasha didn't need telling twice. She and Abi ran off down the road. Flame nestled against Abi, shivering with fright.

The boys ran after them.

"Look!" Sasha pointed across a field. "That's the back of our school. It must be a shortcut!"

Abi spotted a fence. "Over here!" she urged.

She and Sasha climbed up and jumped into the field. Breathing hard, they bounded across the grass. Abi ran as fast as she could, but holding Flame slowed her down. She looked over her shoulder.

Craig was gaining on her!

Sasha reached the gates. She dragged them open and raced toward the school. "We'll be okay now!" she called over her shoulder to Abi.

Abi had one foot inside the gates. Suddenly she was jerked to a halt.

Craig had grabbed her arm!

Abi struggled to pull free. She couldn't push Craig away or she might drop Flame.

Craig's fingers dug into her arm. "Give me that kitten!" he said through gritted teeth.

"No!" Abi winced, her heart pounding. She curled her arms around Flame and struggled to get away, but Craig was too strong.

Flame gave a tiny meow and a couple of silver sparks shot out of his fur. Abi felt a weak tingle up her spine. Flame was feeling better and trying to do some magic.

She gathered all her strength and gave a final wrench. Taken by surprise, Craig lost his grip. Abi made a frantic dive inside the gates.

Behind her, Craig gave a yell. "Help! I'm stuck!"

Abi turned around. Craig's feet seemed rooted in the ground. He shook his knees, trying to make his legs move. She watched his friends run up and grab his hands. They tried to pull Craig free, but he was stuck fast.

"You big bully!" Abi shouted to Craig as she zoomed down the school path after Sasha. She knew the spell would wear off soon.

Abi didn't look back until she was inside the building. Half a minute later, she collapsed against a wall and tried to catch her breath.

"You were brave," Sasha puffed beside her. "That horrible Craig boy was a lot

bigger than you!"

Abi didn't feel brave. Now that the danger was past, her legs felt weak. The scratches on her hands and arms were stinging like crazy, too.

"When did you let that kitten go?" asked Sasha.

"What?" Abi realized that Flame must have made himself invisible. That meant he was feeling back to his old self. "Oh, he jumped down back there in the field," she said quickly. "I bet he lives somewhere close. He'll find his way back. I'm just going up to the room. I want to wash these scratches."

Sasha decided she was hungry and went off to get some sandwiches. "I'll bring some up to the room for you."

"Okay. Thanks. And could you get some milk, please?" Abi began climbing the stairs.

In her room, Abi sat on her bed with

Flame in her lap. He snuggled up close. "You saved me, Abi. Thank you. But are you hurt?" he meowed with concern.

Abi looked at the deep scratches on her hands. She shrugged. "It doesn't matter."

Flame reached out a paw and touched her very gently. Tiny silver sparks, like Christmas glitter, sprinkled her hands and arms. Abi felt them grow warm. The pain faded. Where the scratches had been, there were now just faint marks.

"Thank you, Flame," she said. "I almost died when I saw you up that tree!"

She bent her head and Flame touched her chin with the tip of his cold black nose. A warm glow settled in Abi's heart. She realized how fond she was of the magic kitten. It made her sad to think that one day he may have to leave.

Chapter
SIX

Abi and Sasha were just finishing classes the following day when they were called to Mrs. York's office.

Keera, Tiwa, and Marsha were already there. Marsha's face had gone back to normal.

Mrs. York explained that Mrs. Brown from the store had noticed that some candy had gone missing. "She's positive it was just after the five of you left her store yesterday afternoon. Do you have anything to say?" she asked.

"I had nothing to do with it," Keera said quickly.

Abi's eyes widened. She looked across at Sasha, but by silent agreement neither of them spoke. Abi didn't want to tell on anyone, even if it was Keera and her horrible friends. Sasha obviously thought the same way.

Tiwa and Marsha were also silent.

Mrs. York looked angry and disappointed. "I'm going to give the person responsible a chance to own up. You have until tomorrow morning. After that, I will take steps to find the truth."

In the hallway outside, Keera smirked at Abi and Sasha. She went off with her friends. They heard them laughing together.

Sasha clenched her fists. "Ooh! They make me so mad!" she said. "I really feel like going back and telling the head teacher that Keera took that candy."

Abi frowned. "Me too, but I'm not going to. I hate what Keera did. But I'm not a snitch."

"But we can't let her get away with it!" Sasha said.

"She won't. My mom says that the truth has a way of getting out," Abi said. "Sorry, Sasha, but I really have to go now. It's basketball practice tonight . . ."

"And you still have that project on ancient Egyptians to work on, right?" Sasha guessed. "I was going to computer club, but I can go later. I'll give you a hand."

"Thanks. You're the best friend anyone could have!" Abi linked arms with Sasha.

By the next morning, no one

had owned up to stealing the candy. Somehow the news had gotten out and rumors were all over the school.

"I heard that Mrs. York is going to do a room search," Sasha said to Abi when they were eating lunch. "Maybe Keera will own up before that."

"I wouldn't hold my breath," Abi said. "But I think she might have a guilty conscience."

"How do you know?" Sasha asked.

"She left basketball practice early to go and see the nurse with a headache," Abi replied.

"Did she?" Sasha looked surprised. "I saw her and Tiwa outside our room just before you got back. She seemed okay then."

Just as Abi was finishing her baked potato and salad, she heard someone call her name. "Mrs. York wants to see you," a girl she had seen around school a few times told her.

Abi rose to her feet. She threw a puzzled glance at Sasha. What could Mrs. York want with her?

"Grounded for a week! But I didn't do anything!" Abi burst out.

She stood in her room, looking with dismay at Mrs. York. The head teacher held up three bags of candy, which she had just found under Abi's bed. "Then how do you explain these?"

"But they're not mine," Abi insisted. "Someone must have put them there."

Keera! *She hid the candy under my bed*, Abi thought. That's why she left basketball practice early!

"Please. You have to believe me. I didn't steal that candy," Abi said.

Mrs. York shook her head. "I'm sorry you still can't seem to tell me the truth. I expected more of you, Abi. I'll have more to say about this later." She left the room.

Stung by the unfairness of it, Abi sank onto a chair. How was she going to prove her innocence?

"Caught red-handed, were you?" said a gloating voice from the doorway. "I wouldn't be surprised if they picked someone else to be captain of the basketball team now."

Abi didn't look up. "Just go away,
Keera," she said in a shaky voice.

Over the next week, Abi tried to
throw herself into her schoolwork. But
it was no use. She couldn't seem to
concentrate.

"Keera's telling everyone that you're the thief. We can't let her get away with this!" Sasha fumed at the end of a math class. "I've had enough. I'm going to see Mrs. York right now!"

Abi put her things back into her pencil case. "It's too late for that. Mrs. York will just think you're sticking up for me. She'll never believe me after she found the candy under my bed."

"If only there was some way to make Keera tell the truth," Sasha said.

An idea suddenly sprang into Abi's mind. She sat up straight. "That's it! You're brilliant, Sasha!"

"I am?" Sasha blinked at her.

Abi's idea was taking shape. She grinned. "Remember that first day, how

Keera tried to scare us about the school ghost?"

Sasha nodded. "The Gray Lady."

"Exactly!" Abi said. "I think I might have a way to scare Keera into telling the truth. But I'll need your help."

"Fine. Just tell me what to do," Sasha said.

"Okay. This is the plan . . ."

When Abi had finished, a slow smile spread over Sasha's face. "I think I get the idea!"

That evening, Abi rolled up her bed sheet, tucked it under her arm, and set off with Flame. They made their way along the twists and turns of the old stairways, up to the dusty landing. There

were the narrow windows of thick,
greenish glass that Abi remembered. In
front of her was the ancient wooden
door.

As Abi opened it, it seemed to groan
in protest. She gave a small shiver. It
was even creepier up here than she
remembered, especially in the fading

light.

She wrapped herself in the sheet. "Okay. Do you remember what to do?" she asked Flame.

Flame nodded and gave her a whiskery grin. "I am ready."

Abi heard footsteps on the stairs. "Quick! They're coming!"

She pushed the door so that it almost closed. Slipping the sheet over her head, she melted into the shadows. Little prickles of warmth tickled her spine. Beside her, Flame began to crackle and fizz with silver sparks.

"I'm going back. We're completely lost!" Keera's sulky voice echoed in the stairwell.

"It's just up here, honest. The room's

full of awesome sports equipment," Sasha said. "I found it by accident. No one else knows about it."

"Okay, but you'd better be right about this," Keera warned.

"Wait for it," Abi whispered to Flame.

As Sasha pushed the door wide open, it gave a loud creak.

"Now!" Abi hissed.

She felt herself rising in the air. Higher and higher she floated.

"Whoo-oo-oh!" she wailed, flapping her arms. "Keera Moore. I know you stole that candy," she said in what she hoped was a ghostly voice.

"Aargh!" Keera screamed. "Leave me alone. I'm sorry I stole them!"

"You must own up to what you did,"

Abi said, sounding as spooky as she could.

"All right. Please don't haunt me, Gray Lady!" Keera pleaded.

Abi heard a scuffle and then footsteps running down the stairs. Keera had run away!

"Okay, you can let me down," she whispered to Flame. She drifted down and felt her feet touch the ground. Throwing off the sheet, she gave Flame a quick cuddle. "That was great! Thanks, Flame."

Flame meowed softly. "You are welcome."

Sasha was waiting on the landing when Abi stepped out of the dark room. She grinned broadly. "You were great!

I wish you could have seen Keera's face!
I thought she was going to faint with
fright! Even I was scared. It looked like
you really were floating."

"It must have been a trick of the
light," Abi improvised. "Bet you a week's
allowance that Keera's on her way to see
Mrs. York right now!"

Chapter
SEVEN

Abi and Sasha had a break before the next class. They had taken some drinks and chips outside. It was a warm day and they sat on the grass.

"I can't believe Mrs. York let Keera stay on the basketball team," Sasha said. "And she only got grounded for a couple of days! Just because she put on a big act and went and said sorry to Mrs. Brown at the candy store."

"I know. It doesn't seem fair, does it? I hate to admit it, but we'd really miss having Keera on the team. She's a really good player," Abi said. "Anyway, I'm just happy that my name's cleared."

"Me too. How's basketball going?" Sasha asked.

"Really good. Miss Green's a great teacher. She makes you want to do your best," Abi said. "She says the team's starting to play together as a unit. And she thinks we've got a chance of beating the other schools in the tournament."

"That's great," Sasha said. "It's not that far away, is it?"

Abi shook her head. "No. I can't believe we're halfway through the semester. It's gone by so quickly."

Sasha leaned back on her elbows, enjoying the sunshine. She watched

Keera, Marsha, and Tiwa walk past in the distance.

Abi glanced at Flame. He was chasing a butterfly, batting at it with his front paws. It fluttered away and he rolled over and began biting his tail. She chuckled, feeling a surge of affection for him.

"What are you laughing at?" asked Sasha.

"Oh, nothing," Abi replied.

Sometimes, she forgot that no one else could see Flame. But she never forgot how important it was to keep him a secret. Somewhere out there, fierce cats from Flame's own world were searching for him. And if they ever found him, they would kill him.

The next few weeks passed quickly. Abi hardly had time to think. She concentrated on keeping up with her schoolwork and fitting in basketball practice in any spare moments, and then, one morning, she awoke with a sinking feeling.

"We get our results for our schoolwork today," she whispered to

Flame while Sasha was in the shower. "I just know I'm going to get bad grades."

Flame licked her hand with his rough little tongue. "But you have worked hard," he sympathized.

"I know. I've done tons of extra work. But I'm not sure it'll be enough."

Flame looked up at her with big, round eyes. "I can fix this for you," he meowed helpfully.

Abi shook her head. She tickled his ears. "No. That would be cheating. Thanks, anyway, Flame. But I have to face up to this one myself." She flung back the blanket and jumped out of bed. "Come on. Let's go outside for a walk. There's plenty of time before breakfast."

Flame jumped down eagerly.

Sunshine streamed into the room as Abi put on her school clothes and dragged a brush through her hair. Once outside, she and Flame crossed the soccer field and went toward the woods.

Flame ran around the woods, his ears laid flat to his head. He chased wind-blown leaves and sniffed all the exciting smells in the grass.

Abi relaxed as she smiled at his antics. He loved exploring outside.

She had a sudden thought. "Do you have trees and grass where you come from?"

"Yes. And rivers. And mountains. But no people. Just my kind," Flame told her.

A world with only cats, Abi thought, *how strange that must be*. She would love to see it.

Flame seemed to know what she was thinking. "Magic will take me back to my world one day. I do not know when

but I do know it will only be strong
enough for one," he said sadly.

Abi felt disappointed, but she forced
a smile. "Never mind. I don't suppose
there would be much to eat. I bet you
don't have stores!" she joked.

Flame gave her a whiskery grin. "We do not need stores for juicy prey!"

A piece of silvery paper blew toward Abi. She picked it up and crumpled it into a ball and then threw it across the grass. Flame scampered after it. He rolled over and over, hitting at the paper ball with his front and back paws.

Abi laughed fondly. It was so perfect having Flame here. She didn't want anything to ever change.

Chapter
EIGHT

"Abi, come and look. It's our results!"
Sasha called Abi over to the bulletin board
outside the classroom. They had just
finished a math class.

"What does it say?" Abi hardly dared
look.

"You're tenth out of the whole class.
And you got top grades for your ancient
Egypt project," Sasha read.

"Really? That's fantastic!" Abi's spirits
soared. She felt like she could jump to the
moon.

"You deserve it," Sasha said generously.

"Thanks," Abi said. "But I couldn't have done it without your help. Wow! Look at your grades. You're second in the class. I bet your mom and dad will be really proud."

Sasha blushed, but she smiled. "I'm sure they will. I'm really looking forward to seeing them for the holidays."

Abi nodded. "School's great, isn't it? But I miss my mom and dad, too."

"You'll see them in a few days, won't you? At the basketball tournament?" Sasha reminded her.

"Oh, yes. They're coming to watch. It's going to be great. I'm on my way to practice now. There's only a couple left."

Sasha walked part of the way with her.

She stopped by an open classroom with rows of computers. Sasha was helping to design the programs for the tournament.

"See you later," Sasha said. "Have a good practice."

In the gym, Miss Green chose squads
for a practice match. Abi played in
goal attack position and Keera was goal
shooter. They worked well together on
the court, feeding each other to score
points.

"Well played, you two," Miss Green
said. "Keep up the good work."

Abi and Keera made their way in
silence to the showers afterward. Abi had
enjoyed the game. "You're a really good
player, Keera," she said a bit reluctantly.

Keera looked surprised. "Thanks," she
said. There was a long pause and then she
said quietly, "You're not bad yourself."

Abi blinked at her. Keera was being
almost human! Maybe she really had
learned her lesson and decided to change.

Wait until she told Sasha!

When Abi got back to their room,
Sasha was already there.

"How was computer club?" Abi asked
brightly.

"Oh . . . er, it was okay, thanks." Sasha
had her head down. She reached across to

the bedside table for a tissue and blew her nose.

Abi could tell she had been crying. "What's wrong?"

"I just got a phone call from my mom and dad." Sasha gulped back tears. "They won't be coming home. They have an important business deal to do or something. So I have to stay at school over the holidays."

"Oh, no. What a shame!" Abi sat down next to Sasha and put her arm around her shoulder. "Maybe it won't be so bad. I bet there'll be other girls staying here, too."

Sasha nodded miserably. "I know. But it won't be the same as going home, will it?"

Abi had to agree that it wouldn't.
She would hate to have to stay at school
when semester ended. Poor Sasha.

While she finished eating dinner,
Abi thought about how she could cheer
Sasha up.

The dining room was full of laughter and chatting voices. But Sasha took no notice. She pushed her food around on her plate. It was chocolate pudding, her favorite, but she had eaten only a spoonful.

"Do you want to walk into town?" Abi suggested.

Sasha shook her head. "I don't really feel like it."

Abi tried again. She reached into her backpack. "I've got a great new wildlife magazine. You can read it first, if you like."

Sasha shrugged, but then she took the magazine. "Okay. Thanks."

"I'm worried about Sasha," Abi said

later to Flame. "I really want to make her feel better, but I don't know what to do."

Flame rubbed his head against her chin, making little comforting noises. "Sasha is sad. Magic cannot help her," he meowed.

"No," Abi agreed, petting him gently. "I don't suppose it can."

She frowned, thinking hard. There had to be something she could do. Suddenly an idea came to her. "I've got it! I know what to do to cheer her up!"

Chapter
NINE

When Abi awoke the next day, she couldn't wait to put her plan into action. She would have to speak to her mom and dad about it first, but today was the day of the tournament and they would be here soon. She couldn't wait.

Abi looked out of the window as the first cars arrived. A banner hung over the parking lot entrance. It read: "Welcome to the Brockinghurst School Tournament."

Abi felt really excited. The previous afternoon, the whole school had worked together on getting ready for the festival. She had helped set out chairs in the gym and put up fliers. Sasha had put programs on all the chairs.

Even Keera, Marsha, and Tiwa did their share.

"Those three seem really different," Sasha commented.

"Yes," Abi agreed. She would have loved to explain how Flame had secretly helped her and Sasha to teach them a lesson!

"Should we go down? I'm helping with welcoming and signing-in," Sasha said.

"I'll come down in a minute," Abi said. When Sasha had left, she turned to Flame. "Are you coming to watch the game?" she asked eagerly.

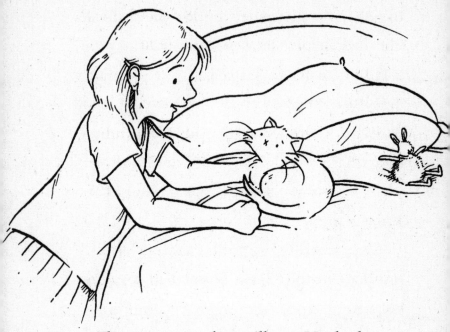

Flame was on her pillow. He had
curled up into a tight ball. "I will stay
here," he decided.

"Really? Won't you be bored?" Abi
looked at Flame in astonishment. Usually
he loved to be where any action was.
She bent down and pet the top of his

head. "I have to go. I promised to help Miss Green set out the cones and stuff for the warm up."

Flame raised his head. His eyes seemed troubled. "Be well, Abi. Be strong," he meowed softly.

"I will be. I'm fine," Abi said. "Don't worry about me."

She gave him a quick cuddle before leaving the room. He seemed in a strange mood.

Just as Abi reached the gym she spotted two familiar figures. They waved at her. "Abi, darling!"

"Mom! Dad!" she cried, flinging herself at them for a hug. "It's so good to see you. I have to ask you something. It's about Sasha . . ."

"Whoa there! Slow down, Abi," Mr. West said with a grin. "Start again from the beginning."

Abi took a deep breath and explained her idea to her mom and dad. She

crossed her fingers, waiting nervously for their response.

They both smiled.

"Sounds fine to me," said Mrs. West. She glanced at her husband. "What about you?"

"I think it's a wonderful idea!" Mr. West ruffled Abi's hair.

"Yes!" Abi did a little dance of joy. "Awesome. Sorry. Got to go and get changed. See you later!"

Abi put on her gym shoes. She was setting out cones on the courts when she spotted Sasha near the team benches.

"Sasha!" she called, hurrying over. "I've got something to tell you. You're not staying here for the school holidays."

Sasha looked surprised. "I'm not?"

"No. You're coming home to stay with me. I asked Mom and Dad and they think it's a great idea. What do you think?"

A big grin spread over Sasha's face. Her dark eyes shone. "That's great! I'd love to come. Thanks, Abi."

"I can't wait. We're going to have an awesome time!" Abi gave Sasha a hug.

Just then a voice came through the loudspeaker. It was time for the tournament to begin.

Chapter
TEN

As Abi fastened her jersey and looked around at Keera and her other teammates, the excitement built up inside her.

"Round one," the loudspeaker announced.

As captain, Abi led her squad to the players' benches. She sat watching as the other schools' squads played. Then it was time for their game.

"Let's play ball!" Abi gave the players high fives.

"Good luck, Abi!" Sasha called from the crowd.

Abi's squad played well. They won
their first match by thirty points to
twenty.

"We're through to the next round!
Great job, girls," Miss Green praised them.

Their next match was more challenging. The squad scraped through by only thirty-six points to thirty-four.

The following rounds were tough, but to Abi's and everyone's delight they managed to win every game that came their way.

Abi flopped onto the team bench, red-faced and sweaty. She gulped a drink as she watched the play-off for third and fourth places.

Finally the loudspeaker rang out. "And now, the finals for this year's inter-school tournament."

Keera stood up. She looked across at Abi. "We can win this," she said.

Abi grinned. "Let's do it!"

As Abi's squad ran onto the court, the

school cheered and waved. "Come on, Brockinghurst!"

Abi played for all she was worth. She scored four baskets and Keera scored five. It was the last minute of the game. Abi jumped high at a catch, but she landed awkwardly and her foot went over the sideline.

The umpire blew her whistle. "Penalty!"

The other squad took the throw-in. They scored a point. It was now fourteen points each.

Abi felt furious with herself. What a stupid mistake.

"It's okay," Keera said generously.

Abi threw Keera a grateful smile, but they still needed to score again to win and there were only a few minutes left to play.

The players regrouped. Abi caught the ball and passed to Keera.

Keera spun around and aimed, but it was a difficult angle. There was only one chance to score. Would she be able to do it?

Abi had a better shot. "To me, Keera!" she called.

Keera looked around.

Abi held her breath. Would Keera give away her chance at a winning goal?

With only seconds to go before the whistle, Keera passed to her. Abi aimed. She scored!

The umpire blew the whistle. Abi's team had won the tournament!

Cheering broke out in the gym. "Abi! Abi!" Abi's classmates chanted her name.

"Well played, Abi," Keera said.

Abi smiled. "You gave me the chance

at the winning shot," she said. She took
hold of Keera's hand and held it up.
"We did it together."

"Abi! Keera!" rang out the cheers.

Keera's cheeks went pink. She gave
Abi a hug. Abi returned it, her face
glowing. "Friends?" she said.

Keera beamed at Abi. "Don't push it!"
she joked.

★

Abi lined up with Keera and the rest
of the squads and Mrs. York presented
the certificates. Afterward, there was a
special snack on the lawn.

Abi showed her certificate to her
parents.

"Great job!" Mrs. West said
delightedly. "And you're doing so well in

class. You seemed to have settled in here really well."

"I wasn't sure I would at first," Abi said. She turned and linked arms with Sasha. "But now I love it here. And I've made some great friends."

Sasha blushed. She grinned from ear to ear.

Suddenly amid all the celebrations, Abi felt uneasy. Something cold prickled up her spine.

She gasped.

Flame! He must be in danger.

She realized now why he had been acting strangely. She knew she had to get to Flame as soon as she could.

"I . . . I have to do something. I'll be right back!" Abi blurted out an excuse to her parents, already racing for a side door.

Somehow she knew just where Flame would be. She wove through the narrow hallways until she came to the staircase. Dashing up the stairs two at a time, she reached the landing. The dusty old door to the storeroom was wide open.

"Flame? Where are you? Are you okay?" Her eyes searched the darkness, looking for the fluffy black-and-white kitten.

"Abi?" came a deep velvety rumble from the shadows.

A large white lion with glowing white fur stepped forward. He smiled, showing long, sharp teeth.

"Prince Flame!" Abi's breath caught in

her throat. She had almost forgotten how startling he was in his true form.

"You're . . . leaving?" she stammered.

Flame nodded. "Cirrus has come to help me."

Now Abi noticed another older-looking lion. He was gray and had a kind, wise face.

"I must go now. Uncle Ebony's spies are very close," Flame growled.

Abi dashed forward. She clung onto Flame and buried her face in his silky white fur. "Take care," she whispered. She forced herself to let him go and backed away.

Flame's fierce emerald eyes crinkled in a smile. "Abi, you are a good friend. Farewell. I will not forget you."

Silver sparks whirled in the air around
the two lions. The sparks spun faster and
faster, like a tornado. Flame raised a paw
in a final wave. His claws glittered like
crystal, and then he and the older lion
were gone.

Abi stared at the empty space, her heart aching.

She would miss Flame so much, but he was safe and that was the most important thing. It had been awesome to share her first semester with the magic kitten. She would never forget all the fun they'd had. It would remain her secret, forever.

Her eyes pricked with tears, but she blinked them away. She had the holidays with Sasha to look forward to. Smiling at the thought, Abi turned and ran down the stairs.